The River
and the Trace

Penn Mullin

High Noon Books
Novato, California

Cover Design and Interior Illustrations: Michael Cincotta

International Standard Book Number: 1-57128-117-7

10 09 08 07 06
2 1 0 9

A number of High Noon Books, like this *Trailblazers
Series*, are particularly appropriate as ancillary social stud-
ies materials. This may explain why the *Postcards Series*
and the *Four Corners Series* are so very popular. Write for
our free High Noon Books catalog that describes these and
many other titles.

Contents

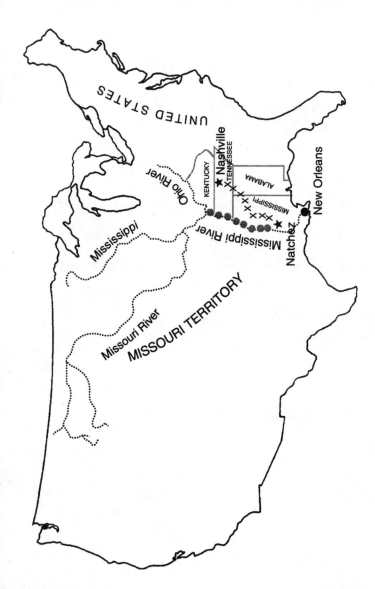

The Mississippi and the Natchez Trace

X = up the Natchez Trace   ● = down the Mississippi River

CHAPTER 1

Mississippi!

"You've been waitin', Bill. Well, there she is –
the Mississippi! You'll be on this river for the
next four weeks! All the way to Natchez!" Curt
told his younger brother. They stood on the deck
of a flatboat. It had just come down the Ohio
River.

Bill stared at the huge wide river ahead. It
made the Ohio look like a creek! "You were
right. It's like an ocean out there. Must be a
mile wide!"

Bill didn't tell Curt what else he thought –
how *small* this boat seemed on this huge river.
Now he was afraid for the first time on the trip.
But for years he had begged Curt to take him
along. And at last Curt had said he was old
enough. It had been a great trip so far.

"Curt! Bill! Grab the sweep! We want to
head straight out!" yelled Nate. He was captain
of the boat. The boys grabbed the long wooden
oar called a sweep. They pulled on it. The man
on the other side of the flatboat pulled on his
sweep, too.

They moved out into the river current.
There were many boats around them now. Most
were flatboats like their own. Fifteen-foot wide

boxes 50 feet long. There was a small hut on deck for shelter. All the boats were stacked with goods to sell in Natchez or New Orleans. Bales of cotton, barrels of pork, flour, salt, beef. Crates of furs, iron, glass.

Curt cheered and threw his hat in the air. "We're on our way now! Straight down to Natchez. Feel how the current just carries us along. All we have to do is watch for sawyers ahead. We saw sawyers on the Ohio, remember, Bill? Trees that stand upside down in the river. Their tops are stuck in the mud. So their trunks and roots stick up in the air. We don't want to hit one of those!"

Nate came up to the boys. "Nope, you can

never trust this river. She'll get you all relaxed and lazy. Then she throws a planter at you."

"What's a planter?" Bill asked.

"It's a tree with its roots jammed in the mud on the river bottom," said Curt. "And the branches are just below the water. You can't see 'em. Those are the nasty ones. They can flip you over."

"The Mississippi keeps changing," Nate said. "Each year she has new surprises for you. You've got to learn about her all over again."

Bill stared ahead at the muddy brown river. What hidden dangers lay beneath that water? They had not worried so much on the Ohio River. But this was a whole new world. He knew it would be his turn to be on watch soon. What if he didn't see a planter in time? The boat would flip over. They'd lose all the cotton Nate had to sell.

Nate seemed to read Bill's mind. "Don't worry. You'll learn the river. Just the way your brother did. How many trips have we made, Curt?"

"This is the fifth, sir," Curt said.

"Well, I don't worry when I've got you aboard," Nate said. Now Nate was speaking in a soft voice. "But there's something about this new feller Jeb. Makes me uneasy. Don't know why. He keeps to himself a lot. But he's sure a good man on the sweeps, that's for sure. Knows the river."

That's strange, Bill thought. I've been feeling uneasy about Jeb, too. There's just something I don't trust about him. He gives Nate angry looks when Nate isn't looking. And he never smiles.

CHAPTER 2

River Camp

"Let's pull in towards shore, boys!" Nate yelled. "There's lots of trees over there. Good place to tie up for the night. We made a lot of miles today."

Bill stared at the far shore. How could Nate see trees? There was just a faint blue blur so far away. But Nate must know. Bill and Curt pulled hard on their sweep. Jeb worked his on the other side. The boat slowly turned in towards shore. Darkness came early now in December. And there was a light chill in the air.

"I sure would love some fresh turkey," Curt said. "The Choctaws might sell us some when we tie up. I hope they have pumpkins, too."

"You best watch out when they come aboard," Jeb yelled. "I don't trust them. No sir! They will see all this cotton we got on board. Then they'll get ideas. We'll never make Natchez."

Bill felt a chill go down his back. He thought the Indians were friendly along the river.

"I've never had trouble with the Choctaws," Curt said. "They've been peaceful. Never any trouble when we're on the Trace going north. I'm more scared of gangs of bandits robbing me then. You meet up with Mason and his boys, and you're in big trouble."

Bill stared at Curt. He had never heard this about the Trace. That was the trail they would walk to get back home from Natchez. Why hadn't Curt ever told him about gangs like Mason's? What else had Curt not told him?

"Pull! Pull!" Nate yelled from his place at the steering oar.

It was hard to keep the boat heading for shore. The strong river current kept pulling it back. Jeb, Bill, and Curt pulled and pulled on the long sweeps. Slowly the boat drew close to the shore. Soon Bill could see the trees. Lots of boats were tied up under them. Huge barges,

Lots of boats were tied up at the shore.

with their masts and sails. Long, narrow keelboats, too. The crew moved these with long poles stuck into the river bottom.

"Hey! Here come some more Kaintucks!" voices called out from shore. "Come tie up over here!"

Bill knew all flatboat men were called "Kaintucks." Even if you were from Tennessee and not Kentucky.

Nate yelled to a man he knew. "Hal! Thought I might see you here! We'll tie up next to you."

Curt threw a rope around a stump on shore. Then he jumped off and tied the boat up tight. The two flatboats were side by side. Hal's was loaded with chairs, beds, and rugs to sell in Natchez. Chickens perched on top of the bedsprings. Dogs ran all over the deck.

Hal jumped aboard their boat. He had a thick gray beard like Nate's and a warm smile. "Well, you got yourself a couple of new boys, don't you, Nate? This one must be Curt's brother. Looks just like him," Hal laughed.

Bill shook hands with Hal. But Jeb just nodded and looked away.

"Looks like you've got a full load," Nate told Hal. "You'll have heavy pockets when you walk north on the Trace."

"I have to sell it all first," Hal laughed. "But I hope you're right! C'mon and join us.

Got rabbit stew tonight. It's all set." He pointed to the campfire on shore.

Soon they were feasting on stew and cornbread. The air was full of songs and laughter.

All of a sudden three dark figures stepped out of the darkness! Tall men wrapped in blankets. The Choctaws. They smiled at the group and opened their sack by the fire. Inside were two large turkeys. "We shoot today. Very fresh," one of them said.

"Just what I wanted!" Curt pulled out money for the Choctaws.

"I'd better buy one, too," Hal laughed. "It's hard to keep my crew happy!" He reached in his pocket and got out his money.

The Choctaws smiled and handed over the turkeys. Then they slipped off into the darkness.

Nate started to sing. Hal joined in. It was an old boatman's song. Bill leaned back against a tree and listened. It was hard to fear the river or the trail home right now. Danger seemed far away. But just then he saw a man standing in the shadows. It was Jeb. Where had he been ever since the boat tied up? Why was he watching them?

CHAPTER 3

Danger on the River

Bill stood on top of the small shed on deck. It was his turn on watch. He looked out at the broad river ahead. All was smooth as glass. But he knew what could be under the water. The boat moved at five miles an hour. Would he have time to see a tree before it flipped them? Curt said to watch for a small break in the smooth water. If you were lucky, this would give you warning.

Nate stood in back at the steering oar. Curt

and Jeb leaned against bales of cotton near their sweeps. Curt trailed a fishing line in the water. Jeb just stared off at the far shore. He talked less and less now. I'll be glad when he leaves in Natchez, Bill thought.

Just then there was a shout. "Hey, Kaintucks!" A big family waved as they drifted by. Their "scow" was made of just logs tied together with a small shed on top. Pigs and goats were aboard, too!

"The new Louisiana territory sure will be full up," laughed Nate. "Look how many scows pass us each day. When did President Jefferson buy it from France – 1803? Been 8 years now and folks have poured in there ever since. This river is gettin' crowded!"

Bill kept his eyes on the river. It was still smooth and clear. He pulled his coat up to cover his neck. The winter wind was cold now.

All of a sudden he saw it. A break in the smooth water ahead. It was coming fast. "Planter! Straight ahead!" he yelled.

Nate pulled hard on the stern oar. Curt and Jeb grabbed their sweeps. Bill froze as he stared at the river. He felt the boat start to turn. And then the branches were under them. One side of the flatboat was lifting. It tipped higher and higher. Bill fell off the shed. He slammed into Curt. Was the boat going over?

Nate yelled, "She'll come down! Hold on!"

17

There was an awful sound of branches scraping the boat bottom. And then a huge jerk as the boat pulled off the tree. They had made it. Bill's heart slammed against his chest. He lay flat on the deck to catch his breath.

"That was a close one," Curt said. "Good thing you warned us, Bill. Gave us time to start our turn. Could have been bad if we'd hit it straight on."

"But we were almost on it when I yelled," Bill said. "It came so fast!"

"That was a hard one to see, Bill." Nate came up to him. "All under the water. You've got a sharp eye!"

"I'll take over watch for awhile," Curt said.

"Maybe you can check the cotton bales, Bill. See if they're still tied down tight."

"This wind will cut down our speed," said Nate. "We won't do our 30 miles today. But we've made good time this trip. We're in the Mississippi territory now. Only 100 miles till Natchez! Just 3 days if we're lucky!"

"You'll have to clean up some when we get there, Bill," Curt laughed. "Or they won't let us in to eat anywhere! And we can't miss Natchez catfish! Best there is!"

All of a sudden Nate let out a yell. "Look what's comin'! Look at the size of her!" He pointed to a huge boat 150 feet long! Smoke was pouring out of the high smokestack as it passed by.

"It's a *steamboat*!" Curt whistled. "They finally made one. Look at her go! It's the NEW ORLEANS on her first trip down the river!"

Even Jeb whistled as she went by.

"This is the end of something, boys," Nate said slowly. "And the start of a whole new time. This means boats can turn around and go back *up* the Mississippi. One day soon we won't have to walk the long Trace back home. We'll ride in one of those steamboats!"

They all stared at the NEW ORLEANS until she steamed out of sight.

CHAPTER 4

Town on the Hill

"Is that it up there?" asked Bill. He stood at the front of the boat with Curt. They were coming in to Natchez. The town spread out over a high hill and down under it, too. More than a hundred boats were tied up at the wharf. Crowds filled the docks and the paths into town. Bill couldn't wait to get off the boat. There would be so many new things to see.

"Let's tie up over there," Nate said. "Then we can unload the boat, and I can pay you boys!" They pulled up to the wharf. It was full of barrels, crates, animals, and people. Buyers called out prices for cotton and furs that had come down the river.

"Sounds as if you'll make lots of money on this cotton," Curt told Nate.

"I hope you're right. Then I will sell the boat. And I'll be all set to start north," said Nate.

Bill saw that Jeb was listening hard while Nate talked. Jeb's eyes darted here and there. It seemed as if he were looking for someone.

They all helped unload the bales of cotton onto the wharf. Then Nate said, "I guess you fellas would like to get paid. Well, you've done

*They all helped unload the bales of cotton
onto the wharf.*

23

a darn fine job. I've never had a better crew. You got this cotton here safe and dry."

Nate took out his money pouch and gave them their pay. He was smiling. "There's a bit extra in there. Curt, don't let Bill spend all his in Natchez!"

"I won't," laughed Curt. "He's got to take some home to Nashville. Say, Jeb, will you stay in Natchez awhile? Or will you start north right off?"

"Don't know," Jeb said. "How about you?"

"Bill and I will start north with Nate after he sells his stuff," Curt said.

"Might see you on the trail." Jeb put his pay in his pocket. "So long!" And then he stepped off the boat onto the wharf. He soon vanished on the crowded dock.

Nate shook his head. "Strange fellow. I just never felt good about him. Glad he's gone now."

"Me, too," Curt agreed.

"I hope we don't see him on the trail north," said Bill.

"Well, you two should get up to town while your clothes still look clean!" Nate said. "I'll sell this cotton. It won't take more than an hour or two. Meet you at the inn later."

"Yes, sir. Get a good price now!" Curt waved and jumped onto the wharf with Bill. They set off into the crowd.

There was so much to see. Shops full of

pies, hats, boots, fancy clothes. Inns where you could smell meat grilling. Shops with sweets in the window. Bill kept his hand on the money in his pocket. He'd never had so much in his life – 50 dollars! He'd take some home to Ma. But first he'd spend just a bit here. Maybe a new knife. A warm shirt for the trip north. They stopped at a shop window. Just then Bill saw something out of the corner of his eye. Was it Jeb watching them?

CHAPTER 5

The Natchez Trace

They were on their way home. Five hundred miles through the wilderness. Swamps, bugs, rats, cougars, and the gangs of bandits. Bill looked into the dark woods on both sides of the trail. Were they being watched? Was Mason out there with his gang? Nate had a lot of money with him. He got a good price for his cotton and the flatboat. His rifle was always on his shoulder now.

They had joined up with five other

boatmen. It was good to be in a group if you met up with bandits. You had more of a chance then.

It was a happy bunch. They all had money in their pockets. They sang, told stories, bragged a lot, walked fast. The trail was never straight. It twisted and turned to miss swamps and creeks.

"This is an old Choctaw trail," Nate told Bill. "And before them, animals used it. So it goes back a long time. Jefferson made a treaty with the Choctaws so we could use their trail. You'll see lots of them on this trip."

"Straight ahead," said Curt. "The Choctaws run the ferry over the river."

Bill looked at the small raft for their group and two pack horses. Could it hold them all? But the Choctaws rowed them safely across and sold them sweet potatoes for supper.

The dark came early on these winter nights. Soon it was time to make camp in the woods. The fire seemed to push away the black night. So they all stayed near it. Some of the men like Nate buried their money in holes for the night. They weren't taking any chances. Bill thought about Mason's gang a lot when night came.

"This rabbit you shot is good!" Nate told Curt. "I'll send you out to hunt every day!"

They had roasted the rabbit on a stick above the fire. There were wild berries, dried

29

biscuits, and the sweet potatoes, too.

One of the men brought out his fiddle. There were long soft songs around the fire. Then they laid down their blankets. They slept with their heads on their knapsacks. Many hands held rifles.

CHAPTER 6

Smith's Stand

Bill woke up with a start. A rider was in their camp. His horse had been running hard. Who was it?

"Mail rider!" Curt sprang to his feet. "Hey, feller! We've got water for your horse. Stay for breakfast with us."

"I'll take the water, thanks. No time to eat. I've got to make Natchez tonight," the man said. He pointed to his saddlebags. "Big load of mail."

All the men gathered around the rider. There were lots of questions. "How's the trail ahead? Is the river high? Have you heard any word of bandits?"

"That Mason gang. Heard they're on the Trace all right. Keep a sharp eye," the rider said.

Bill felt a chill go down his spine. He looked off into the dark woods. Were they being watched even now?

The mail rider raced off down the trail. Then the men ate a cold breakfast of dried beef and biscuits.

Nate dug up his money pouch. "That Mason best not tangle with us," he said. "He'll wish he hadn't."

That day the trees hung over the Trace. It was like a green tunnel. The group moved fast. The sooner they got to Nashville, the better. No one wanted to lose his money.

At noon they came to a clearing in the woods. A large log cabin stood there. Horses were tied up outside. "This is Smith's Stand," Nate told Bill. "He takes in people for the night. Serves food, too. We'll go in and get a bite. And we're getting low on supplies. We can buy some coffee and flour."

It was dark and smoky inside. The rooms were full of men eating and laughing. There was hot squirrel stew for lunch with fresh bread and milk. Bill ate till he could barely move. "Will we stay in one of these stands some nights?" he asked Curt.

"If there's a storm we will. Otherwise it's better outside." Curt spoke in a soft voice. "These stands are full of spies. They find out how much money you've got. Word gets out."

Bill looked at the other men in the stand. They looked the same as he did. Their clothes were torn and dirty. They were bearded and sunburned from the long river trip. Which ones might be the spies?

The door opened. In came a group of soldiers. Even their uniforms were dirty and worn from the long trail. "They're on their way

34

south," Nate said, "to protect the new lands we just got from France."

"Surveyors here, too," said Curt. "Going down to map all that new land."

"This is the only road south right now," Nate said. "It sure is busy. Well, I'd better go buy that coffee and flour. It's time we got back on the trail."

The days went by fast. Soon the second week was gone. There was no rain, so they slept out each night.

Sometimes they ate at the stands along the trail. Most were 20 miles apart. Choctaws ran a lot of them. The men often bought the rough bread they sold. It was called *kuntee* (kun-TEE).

Bill began to think about home. His own bed. Ma's pies and roasts. Only one more week or so if all went well. Maybe Curt would let him come on the trip next fall, too. First the river, then the Trace.

It was close to dark. Time to make camp. "You boys take my gun and shoot us some squirrels for supper!" Nate said. "I'll start the fire."

CHAPTER 7

The Sound of Horses!

Bill and Curt set off into the woods. "We better shoot fast. Not much light left," Curt said. They walked on. Soon there was no light left.

"Nate will have to eat corn mush tonight," Bill laughed. "The squirrels have gone to bed."

They started back to the camp. The woods were silent and dark now.

All of a sudden Curt jerked Bill back. He pointed to the camp. Bill could see three new horses. Whose were they? At first the boys did not move. Then slowly they crept forward and crouched behind some bushes. They could hear voices.

"We know how much you fellas have on you," said a rough cruel voice.

"Where's the cotton money, Nate?" Bill knew that voice. It was *Jeb*! "Mason, Nate's got it. I know he has."

Mason! Bill's heart slammed hard in his chest. He and Curt looked at each other. This was as bad as it could be. Except for one thing. They each had a rifle. But what if Jeb wondered where they were? What if he came looking for them?

Mason grew meaner now. "O.K., Nate. I'll give you one more chance. Where are you

*Then they crept forward and crouched
behind some bushes.*

hiding the money?"

Stall, Nate, stall, Bill thought to himself. Give us time to get closer. He and Curt inched forward. Mason stood with Jeb and one more man facing the fire. Mason was huge and cruel looking. He had an evil smile.

"Jeb, I knew you were a rat. You were working for Mason all along," said Nate. He was stalling.

"When I count to three we stand up," Curt whispered. "One, two . . . three!" They stood up. "Drop the guns, Mason!" Curt yelled. "We've got you covered!" He and Bill stepped out of the bushes.

"What the . . . " sputtered Mason. He and

his two men dropped their rifles.

"Nate, take their guns," Curt said.

Bill tied the bandits' hands. I'm touching Mason, he thought, trembling.

"The marshal will be real glad to see you guys," Nate said. "I hear there's a reward out for you."

He turned to Bill and Curt. "Lucky for us you two went out to shoot squirrels. You're brave boys. And you've caught yourselves the famous Mason!"

"Where's the rest of your gang?" Curt asked Mason. Lucky there were only three of you here, he thought. We never could have taken the whole gang.

Mason did not answer.

They took turns guarding the prisoners all night. Each noise in the woods made them jump with fear. Was it Mason's gang come to rescue him? They were all glad when dawn came.

"We'll let the prisoners walk," Nate said. "We'll ride their horses."

"You'll never get us to the marshal," Mason snarled at Nate.

Bill felt a chill go down his spine.

They started up the Trace. The dark woods closed in on either side of them. Were they being watched? Nashville was still a week away.

All of a sudden they heard the sound of

horses behind them!

"Get off the trail!" Nate yelled. "Into the woods!" They pulled the prisoners with them into the bushes.

The riders came closer. Bill peered out to see them. He saw blue coats! Soldiers! Not Mason's gang!

Nate ran out on the trail and waved his arms. The soldiers stopped.

Curt and Bill led the prisoners out of the woods.

"Mason!" said the head soldier. "The Terror of the Trace. How did you get him? And two of his gang?"

Nate smiled. "We got lucky. I have two

boatmen who went out squirrel hunting. And look what they got!" He pulled Curt and Bill forward proudly. "These boys get the reward!"

"And it will be a big one," the soldier said. "We'll take Mason and his boys to the Nashville marshal. We'll tell them who gets the reward. The Trace will sure be safer now!"

"I hope you two will still be my boatmen next fall," Nate told Curt and Bill. "All that reward money. Will you still want to go down the river?"

Bill and Curt both laughed. "Nate, the reward is yours, too! And don't go down the river without us! We'll all spend the reward when we get back to Natchez!"